James Mayhew
presents

Ella Bella
BALLERINA
~ and ~
Swan Lake

8/13
E
Mayhew

For Lesley Agnew
~ Bookseller extraordinaire ~
and
for Rosalind Sippy
~ Also a Wonderful bookseller ~
(and ballet costumier)
With thanks and love
J. M.

First edition for North America published in 2011
by Barron's Educational Series, Inc.

Text and illustrations © James Mayhew 2010

First published in 2010 by Orchard Books
338 Euston Road
London, NW1 3BH

All inquiries should be addressed to:
Barron's Educational Series, Inc.
250 Wireless Boulevard
Hauppauge, New York 11788
www.barronseduc.com

ISBN: 978-0-7641-6407-1

Library of Congress Catalog Card No.: 2010936559

Date of Manufacture: March 2013
Manufactured by: South China Printing Co., Dongguan, China

Printed in China
9 8 7 6 5 4 3 2

James Mayhew
presents

Ella Bella
BALLERINA
~ and ~
Swan Lake

It was pouring rain when Ella Bella arrived at
the old theater for her ballet lesson.
"Come in, darling," said Madame Rosa, her
ballet teacher. "It's lovely and warm inside."

Ella Bella changed into her
ballet shoes and joined
the rest of the class.

"Now, my darlings," said Madame Rosa, fetching her music box, "today we shall dance to the music from *Swan Lake*." "That's a pretty name for a ballet," said Ella Bella. "Does it have any princesses?"

"Of course!" exclaimed Madame Rosa. "There is a swan princess!"

Inside the beautiful box, the little ballerina spun
around and magnificent music began to play.
The children all imagined they were baby swans
as they danced around the stage.

"Will you tell us about the swan princess?"
asked the children.
"Well, her name is Odette," said Madame Rosa.
"A wicked sorcerer turned her into a swan and only
at night was she allowed to be a princess again."

"Couldn't the spell be broken?" asked Ella Bella.
"Only with the promise of true love," replied
Madame Rosa. "And one night, Odette met a
handsome prince, but the wicked sorcerer tried
to stop them from falling in love . . ."

Just then, the music finished.
"Goodness! Time to get
changed, children," called
Madame Rosa. "Off we go."
But Ella Bella stayed behind
on the big empty stage,
all by herself.

Gently, she lifted the lid
of Madame Rosa's music box.
The little ballerina inside began
to twirl. Then, the *Swan Lake*
music played and, as Ella Bella
danced around, it grew louder
and louder!

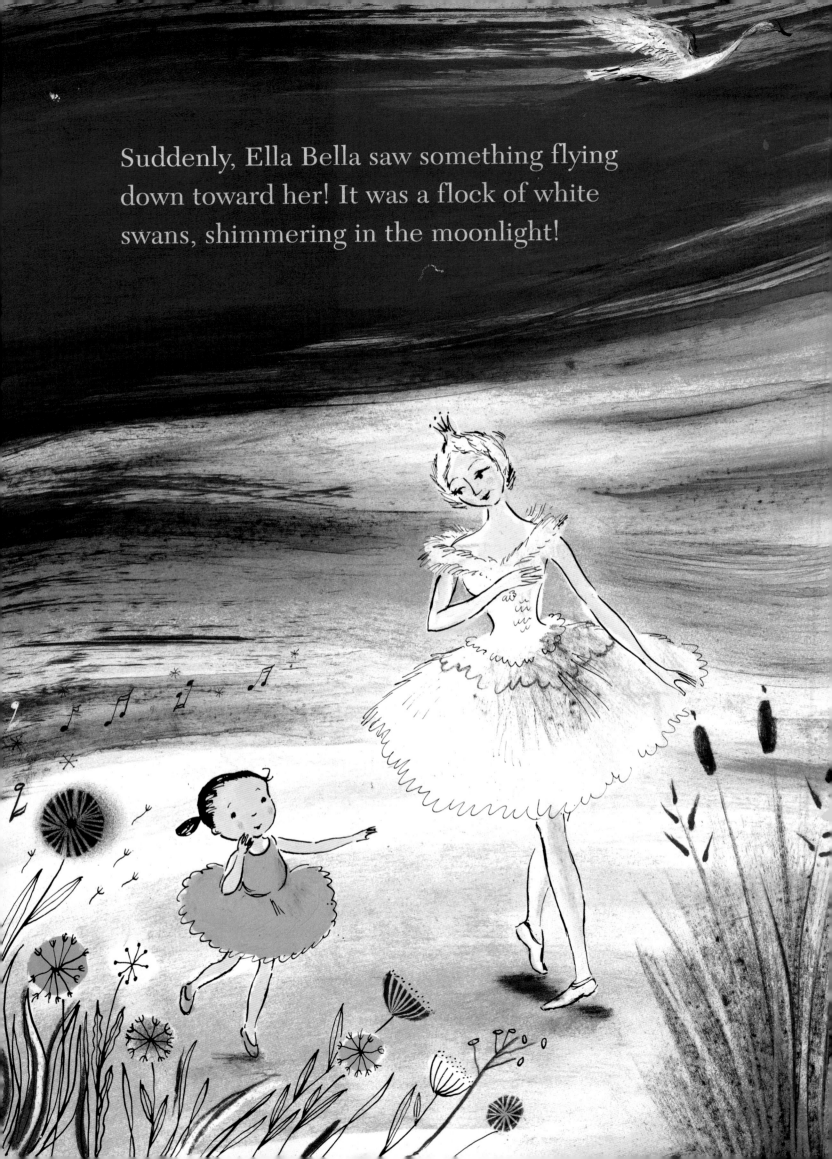

Suddenly, Ella Bella saw something flying down toward her! It was a flock of white swans, shimmering in the moonlight!

As they landed beside a lake, the swans turned into
beautiful ballerinas. One of them wore a crown.
"You must be the Swan Princess!"
said Ella Bella, curtseying.

"Yes, I'm Princess Odette," the Swan Princess whispered shyly. "And my beloved prince is waiting at the castle. He promised to declare his love for me at the Royal Ball tonight!"
"Would that break the sorcerer's spell?" asked Ella Bella.

"It would," said Odette, "but if
the sorcerer finds out, he will try to
stop the prince from declaring his love."
"Let's make sure the sorcerer isn't
there," said Ella Bella. "I'll go with you."
They set off for the castle together.

Ella Bella left Odette outside and stepped into the
dazzling ballroom. She could see no one who looked
like a sorcerer. Instead, an amazing sight met her eyes!

Princesses from all over the world danced for
the prince. But he seemed to be waiting for
someone special . . .

Just then, a tall baron in a long feathery cape
arrived with another princess. She looked exactly
like Odette, but she was dressed in black, and
her eyes flashed as she looked at the prince.
"Please, may I have this dance?" he asked her.
"That *can't* be Odette," thought Ella Bella.
"She was wearing white!"

Ella Bella greeted the prince.
"Excuse me, Your Highness . . ." she began.
But the prince didn't seem to hear her.
"I give this princess my promise of true love!"
he declared.

"But look!" said Ella Bella, pointing.
The prince suddenly saw the real Odette,
fluttering helplessly at the window!

The baron began to laugh. He revealed that
he was the sorcerer and he had cast a magic spell
to make his daughter, Odile, look like Odette!

Ella Bella and the prince rushed outside, but Odette had vanished! They quickly ran down to the lake to search for her.

They found Odette hiding in the reeds with the other swan-maidens.

"You've promised your love to another," she wept.
"At sunrise I will become a swan forever!"
"But I was tricked by the sorcerer," said the
prince. "It's you I love. We must never part
again!"

But just then, the angry sorcerer appeared!
He summoned a terrible storm to keep
the prince and Odette apart.

Odette leapt into the lake to
escape the sorcerer's clutches.

The prince fought with the sorcerer and threw him to the ground before bravely leaping after Odette!

The storm cleared and, as the sun rose, Ella Bella saw Odette in the arms of the prince. Even though it was morning, she had not turned into a swan!

"True love has destroyed the sorcerer's magic!" exclaimed Odette. "Thank you, Ella Bella, and farewell!" Music filled the air as Ella Bella watched Odette and the prince sail across the lake, happy and in love.

Ella Bella twirled around . . . but realized the music had stopped. She was all alone on the empty stage. Ella Bella slowly closed the lid of the music box.

"Are you still here?" said Madame Rosa, peeping around the doorway. "Your mother is waiting for you."

Ella Bella told Madame Rosa about Odette and her prince.
"It's a beautiful story," said Madame Rosa.
"I'm sure they lived happily ever after."
"Of course they did!" laughed Ella Bella.

"Now, good night my little swan-girl,"
said Madame Rosa. "Don't forget to practice
your dancing."

"I won't," said Ella Bella. "Good night!"
And she danced and splashed in the puddles
all the way home, just like a baby swan.

Swan Lake is the most famous classical ballet in the world.

Its beautiful and haunting music was written by the great Russian composer Peter Tchaikovsky. The idea was inspired by a children's ballet called *The Lake of Swans,* which he wrote for his niece and nephew to perform at home. Then, in 1875–1876 Tchaikovsky turned it into a ballet with four acts for the magnificent Bolshoi Theatre in Moscow, Russia.

Swan Lake was Tchaikovsky's very first ballet. At first, some people thought it was too hard to dance to the music and it was only after Tchaikovsky's death that *Swan Lake* became truly successful. In 1895, the choreography (ballet steps) and the story were changed, and a new performance took place in St. Petersburg, Russia. This time the ballet was a triumph.

Over the years, new ideas have been added and now lots of different versions of the story exist. Sometimes there is a tragic ending where the prince (who is named Siegfried) and Odette are reunited in heaven. Often the wicked baron (who is named Von Rothbart) can use magic to turn himself into an owl, and Odile, his daughter, into a black swan.

Odette and Odile are performed by the same dancer. Nowadays, every great ballerina longs to play the double role of the white and black swans. Although it's a very challenging part that requires great strength, a talented ballerina can be as graceful and elegant as a real swan.